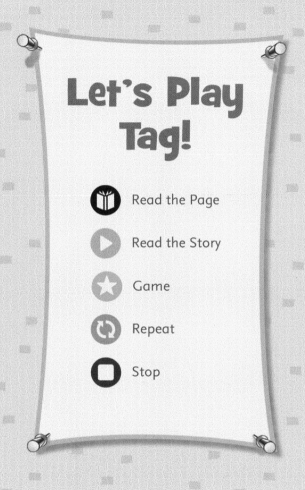

Let's Play Tag!

 Read the Page

▶ Read the Story

★ Game

🔄 Repeat

⬛ Stop

INTERNET CONNECTION REQUIRED FOR AUDIO DOWNLOAD.
To use this book with the Tag™ Reader you must download audio from the LeapFrog® Connect Application.
The LeapFrog Connect Application can be installed from the CD provided with your Tag Reader or at leapfrog.com/tag.

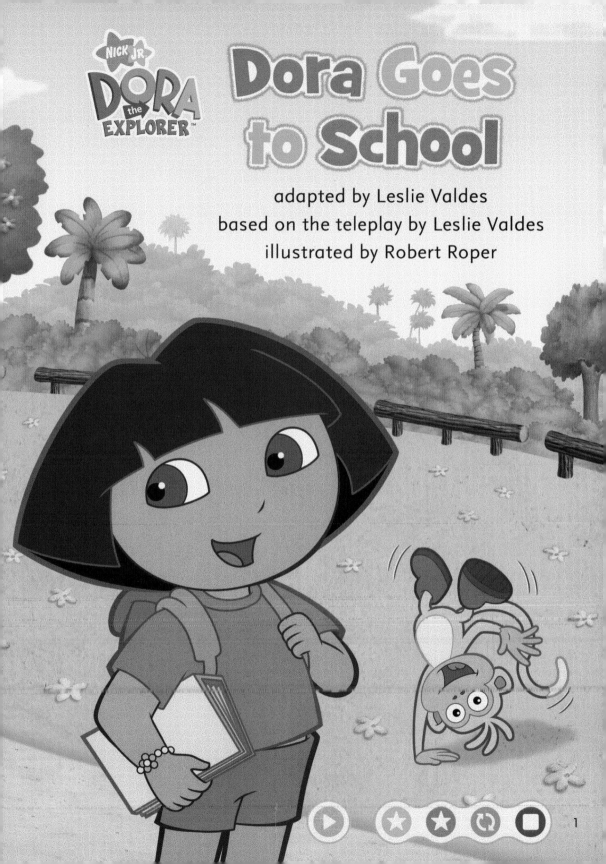

Dora Goes to School

adapted by Leslie Valdes
based on the teleplay by Leslie Valdes
illustrated by Robert Roper

¡Hola! I'm Dora and this is my best friend, Boots. It's our first day of school today! And look, there's our teacher, Maestra Beatriz! She's on her way to school too.

Maestra Beatriz has to get to school before the students do, but her bicycle just got a flat. We have to help her get to school fast!

First, she needs us to help carry her school supplies. Where can we put her supplies? Yeah! Backpack can carry them.

Now let's find the quickest way to school. Who do we ask for help when we don't know which way to go? We can ask Map!

Map says we need to go through Letter Town, over Number Mountain, and that's the quickest way to get to school.

I hear the first school bell. We need to get to school before the third bell. We'd better hurry!

Do you see something that can take us through Letter Town fast? *Sí. El autobús* will take us through the town. *¡Vámonos!*

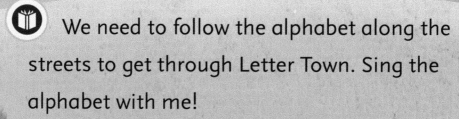

We need to follow the alphabet along the streets to get through Letter Town. Sing the alphabet with me!

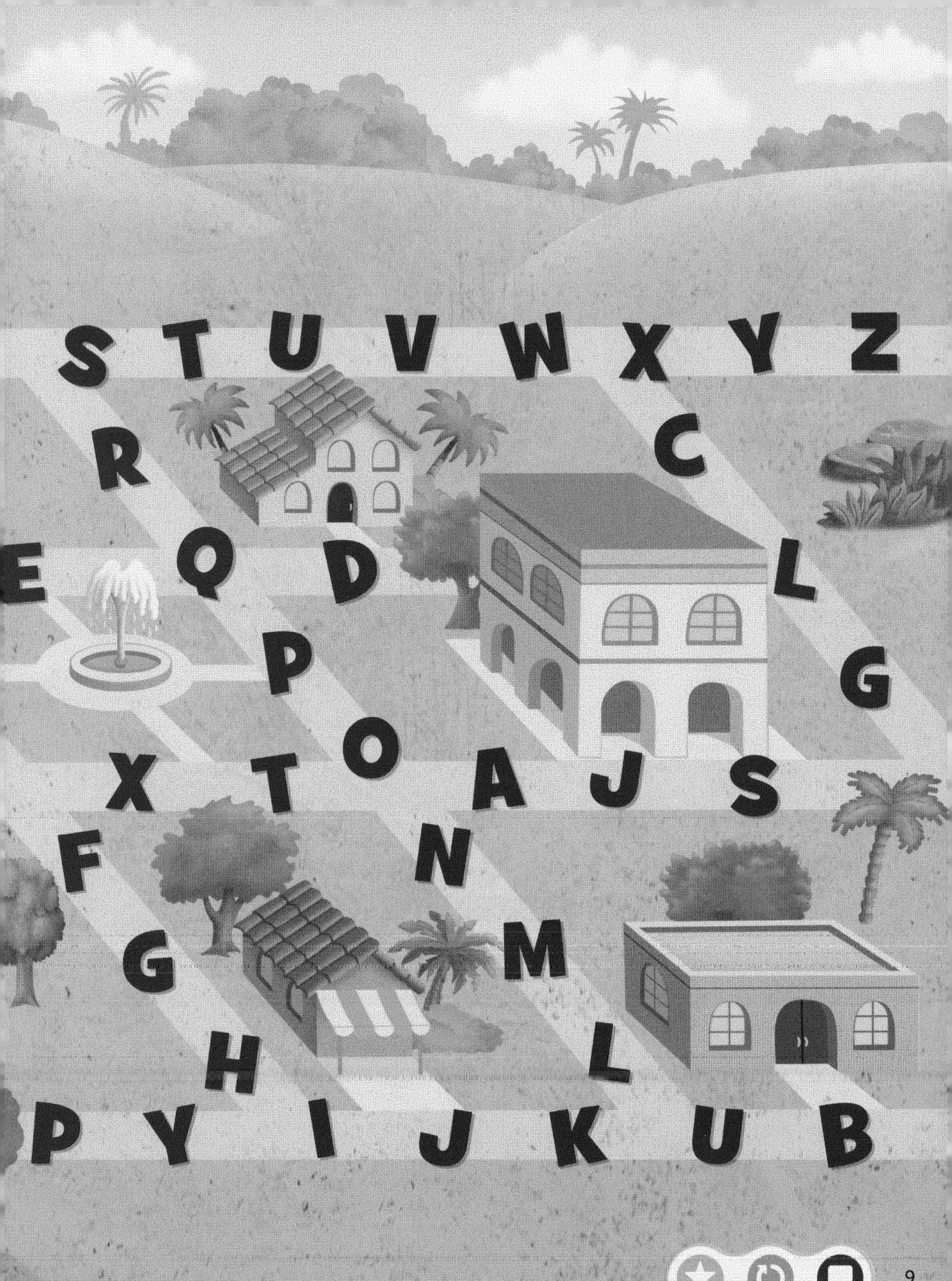
S T U V W X Y Z
R C
E Q D L
P G
X T O A J S
F N
G M
H L
P Y I J K U B

Uh-oh, I hear the second school bell. We really need to hurry! *¡Rápido!* I see some mountains up ahead. Which one is Number Mountain?

We made it to Number Mountain! Who can give us a ride over it? Our friend Azul the train! *¡Sí!*

To ride over Number Mountain we have to count the numbers. Count with me: 1, 2, 3, 4, 5, 6, 7, 8, 9, 10. That's great!

Now let's count backward as we ride down the other side: 10, 9, 8, 7, 6, 5, 4, 3, 2, 1. Yay! We made it over Number Mountain.

There's the school! But to get there we need to cross the forest. Here comes my cousin Diego. He says the condors can fly us over the forest.

Will you help us call the condors so we can get to school superfast? You need to say, "Squawk, squawk!" Say it louder!

Good calling! Now we can ride the condors all the way to the school. You need to hold on tight. Whee!

We made it to school! Now we have to run inside and set up the classroom before the other students come in.

Will you check Backpack to find Maestra Beatriz's school supplies?

Yay! We found Maestra Beatriz's school supplies, but I hear Swiper! That sneaky fox will try to swipe them! We have to say, "Swiper, no swiping!" Say it with me: "Swiper, no swiping!"

Thanks for helping us stop Swiper! Look, here come Maestra Beatriz's other students.

"Good morning, class!" says Maestra Beatriz.

"*¡Buenos días!*" say the students.

I hear the third school bell! Thanks for helping us get to school on time!

The End.

beginning middle end

So Many Books!

Field Trip to the Museum

beads

statue

pottery

headdress

archaeologist

skeleton

tapestry

topaz

shard

mask

29